# William and the mouse



William and Hamid were playing with William's new mouse, Eenor.

'Why is he called Eenor?' asked Hamid.

'Work it out,' said William.

'I can't,' frowned Hamid.

'Look at the size of him,' said William. 'He's enormous. Eenor Mouse. Get it?'

'Are you allowed to have Eenor Mouse in the house?' asked Hamid.

'I'm not supposed to,' replied William, 'but Mum won't know. She won't be back for ages.'

William opened Eenor's cage and let him climb up inside Hamid's sleeve. 'Get him out,' laughed Hamid. 'He's tickling me.'

William put Eenor on the rug and the two boys watched him explore. 'He's enjoying himself,' said William. 'It must be boring, having to stay in a cage all day long.'

Suddenly, Eenor darted under the chair. 'Oh no!' said William. 'Don't let him get away!' He started to move the chair but Hamid stopped him. 'Be careful!' he said. 'Don't squash Eenor!'

The two boys lifted up the armchair but there was no sign of the mouse. 'Put this chair on top of the other one,' said William, 'so he has nowhere to hide. We'll have to find Eenor before Mum gets back.'

'Perhaps he's hiding under the rug,' suggested Hamid. 'He must be in this room somewhere. The door is closed.' William and Hamid rolled up the rug but there was no sign of Eenor. They put the rug on top of the two chairs.

'I'll bet he's under the sofa,' said Hamid.

William pulled all the cushions off the sofa and put them on the table. Then he and Hamid turned the sofa on its side and looked in the stuffing.

'If he's gone in there, we'll never find him,' said Hamid. 'Perhaps he's behind the shelves.' They started to take everything off the shelves. Soon there were books, records, photographs, plants and ornaments all over the floor.

William was getting worried. 'We must search everywhere,' he said. 'Mum will be home soon, and if she finds out that I've had Eenor in the house, I'm in big trouble.' They looked in the waste-paper basket, and in the sideboard. They looked behind the television and behind the curtains. Then they started all over again.

'I know!' shouted William. 'We'll get some cheese. We'll put it in the middle of the floor, and when Eenor comes out to nibble it, we'll catch him!'

William and Hamid ran to the kitchen. William was taking a big piece of cheese from the fridge when his sister, Julie came in. 'What are you up to with that cheese?' she asked. 'Mum will be home in a minute and it will be dinner time.'

'I just wanted to look at it,' said William.

Julie looked as if she didn't believe him. 'I think you're up to something,' she said. 'What have you been doing?'

'Nothing,' said William.

'I'll go and see,' said Julie.

'Now we're for it,' whispered Hamid.

After a minute or two Julie came back into the kitchen. She was carrying Eenor in his cage. 'I think you had better take Eenor out into the shed, where he belongs,' she said. 'If Mum finds out you've had him indoors there'll be trouble.'

'But where was he?' asked Hamid.

'In his cage,' replied Julie, 'going round and round in his little wheel.'

William and Hamid took Eenor out into the shed. 'That was close!' said Hamid. 'That's the only place we didn't look.'

'There's no place like home,' said William. 'He must have run back to his cage when he saw us moving the furniture about.'

'Oh no!' gasped Hamid.

'The sitting room!' groaned William. 'What's Mum going to say when she sees it?'

At that moment the boys heard the click of the garden gate. Mum came up the garden path and went into the house. 'Wait for it,' whispered William.

# 'William!'

## All about mice

The most common mice in Europe are the House mouse and the Long-tailed fieldmouse, sometimes called the Woodmouse. A long time ago the first mice lived in China but now mice are to be found all over the world. Mice usually live close to places where human beings live. A House mouse is a greyish-brown colour and weighs about as much as a 10p piece. House mice depend on humans for all their food. They like grain and scraps of human food best, but they will eat almost anything. They make their holes anywhere in houses. They gather scraps of wool, paper and straw and put these into their nests to make them soft. House mice are very timid and usually come out at night to see what they can find.

A House mouse can have five sets of babies a year. A set of baby mice is called a litter. There are usually five or seven babies in each litter. This means that one House mouse can have as many as thirty five babies a year but not all of them survive.

Mice carry germs so it's unhealthy to let them go anywhere near food.
They can chew through electric cables and cause house fires.

Fieldmice are a little bigger than House mice and are reddish-brown with a white belly. They are found in gardens, fields, and hedgerows in the country. They make their nests in burrows, underneath hedges or in fields. Fieldmice eat almost anything. They store corn, nuts and seeds for the winter, in their burrows. They are very timid and when they are frightened, they sit up and wash themselves all over.

Harvest mice are tiny animals. They are a bright reddish-brown colour with a white belly. In summer they are often seen in cornfields. They use their tails to swing from corn stalk to corn stalk. They are very playful animals and enjoy doing gymnastics. During the cold months of winter they stay in their nests and sleep. They like to eat grain, flies and insects.

## Yin Ling's tale

Yin Ling's class had been doing a project about mice. They had read stories about mice, drawn pictures of mice, and written poems about them. 'This weekend,' said Miss Macintosh, 'I want you to write a story about a mouse.'

'Oh no!' said Yin Ling. 'We've been doing mice for days. There's nothing left to write about.'

'That's true,' said Karen. 'We've read about mice helping lions to escape, country mice visiting town mice, the Pied Piper, and the Tailor of Gloucester.'

'I've got lots of books about mice,' said Yin Ling. 'I'm going to look at them all again and try to imagine what it's like to be a mouse. Then I'll write my story.'

That evening, Yin Ling read all her mouse books before she went to bed. 'I still can't think of anything to write,' she thought. 'I'll try again in the morning.'

When Yin Ling woke up next morning she had grown long whiskers and a tail. She wasn't in her own bed. She was in a nest made of wool and bits of old newspaper.

'So this is what it feels like to be a mouse,' she thought. 'I suppose I'd better go and find some breakfast. I'm feeling very hungry.'

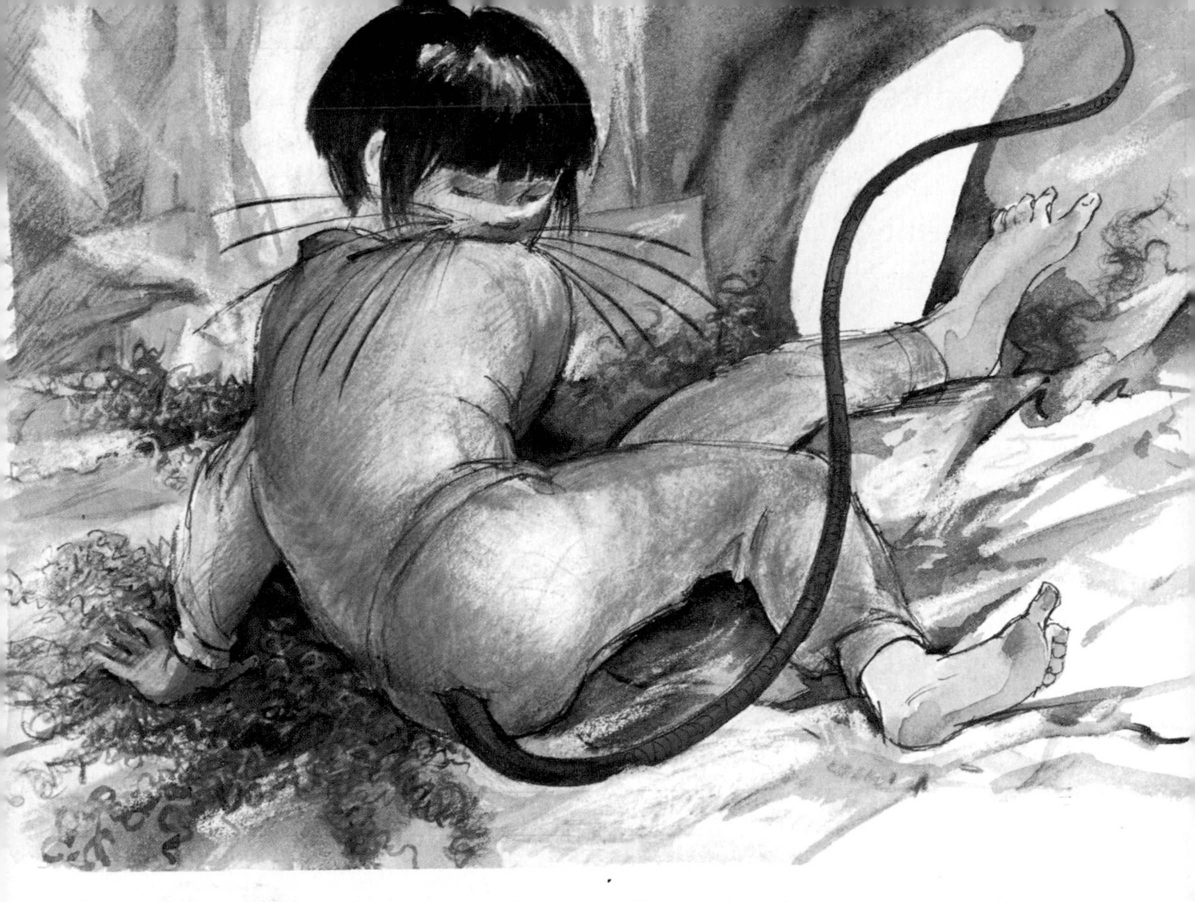

Instead of Yin Ling's bedroom door, with her blue dressing gown hanging on it, there was a small hole in the wall. It was just big enough for her to squeeze through. She went through the hole and found herself in an enormous room. 'I wonder where I am,' she thought.

There was a delicious smell in the enormous room. 'It smells like breakfast,' thought Yin Ling. She walked and walked until she came to a small table and chair. On the table were toast and marmalade, orange juice and coffee, and a boiled egg in an egg-cup. 'Just what I need!' squeaked Yin Ling. 'Somebody must be expecting me.'

Yin Ling was just about to sit down on the little chair when 'Stop!' squeaked a voice behind her. 'Don't sit down!'

'Who's there?' shouted Yin Ling. 'You made me jump. Where are you?'

A boy came from behind what looked like a tall tree. He was just like an ordinary boy, except that he had whiskers and a tail, just like Yin Ling.

'Don't go near the table,' he said.

'I'm sorry,' said Yin Ling. 'I didn't know it was your breakfast.'

'It isn't breakfast,' said the boy. 'Watch.' He took a rubber ball from his pocket and threw it on to the table.

As the ball hit the table, there was a loud pinging noise and a great iron bar crashed down on to the food. The chair and the table were squashed flat. 'You see,' smiled the boy. 'It was a trap.'

'What a nasty thing!' gasped Yin Ling. 'Who could have done that?'

'Don't say you've never seen a mouse-trap before,' said the boy. 'They're all over the place. You'll have to be very careful if you don't want to be caught in one.'

'But why should anybody want to trap me?' asked Yin Ling.

'Because you're a mouse,' said the boy.

Yin Ling began to twitch her tail. 'I don't think I want to be a mouse any more,' she said. 'I want to go home.'

'It's not so bad when you get used to it,' smiled the boy. 'Come on! Let's go and find something to eat. The kitchen is the best place.'

Yin Ling followed the boy to the kitchen. It seemed a very long way away. She was quite tired by the time they arrived. In the kitchen was a giant cupboard. One of its doors was partly open. 'This is the place,' whispered the boy. 'There's usually plenty to eat here. The door is always open because the hinge is broken.'

'Look at all this food!' gasped Yin Ling. There were packets of chocolate biscuits as big as lighthouses, jelly cubes as big as cars, raisins the size of cushions, and nuts the size of rowing boats. They were just about to start on the chocolate biscuits when Yin Ling said, 'In all the mouse stories I've ever read this is the moment when a cat comes in.'

The boy dropped the raisin he was holding and let out a squeak. 'Look!' he cried. 'You've done it now. You shouldn't have mentioned the cat.' Through the gap in the cupboard door Yin Ling saw a great yellow eye staring down at her like the moon.

'Quick!' squeaked the boy. 'Get behind the tins of cat food. She may not have seen us.'

'I think she has,' squeaked Yin Ling. At that moment an enormous ginger paw snaked its way into the cupboard. Yin Ling and the boy threw themselves behind a row of tins. 'Oh no,' said Yin Ling. 'I think she's pulling the door open.'

The ginger cat managed to open the cupboard door and looked at the six tins of cat food on the shelf. She got her paw behind the first tin and flicked it down on to the floor. Yin Ling and the boy held their breaths and huddled together at the end of the row. They had no way of escape. The ginger cat got her paw behind the second tin and flicked it down on to the floor.

Yin Ling and the boy watched helplessly as the third tin fell. Then the fourth, and the fifth. They had only one tin left to hide behind and nowhere to run.

The enormous ginger paw came round the last tin towards the two children. Yin Ling saw the white claws scratch against the label.

'Now I know what it feels like to be a mouse,' whispered Yin Ling. 'And I don't like it one bit.' The last tin fell to the floor. Yin Ling and the boy saw the two huge yellow eyes rise like suns over the shelf. The cat's nose twitched. Its pink tongue licked its white teeth as it got ready to pounce.

Yin Ling saw the paw coming towards her. It felt soft and furry as it tried to pull her off the shelf. 'I'm not a mouse! I'm not a mouse!' she screamed.

'I should hope you're not,' said Yin Ling's mum. 'Come on, get up. The cat has made a terrible mess in the kitchen cupboard during the night. There's cat food, biscuits, and rice all over the floor. When you have had your breakfast you can help me clear up the mess. We really must mend that broken hinge on the cupboard door.'

## The mouse's marriage

Once, in China, there lived a rich mouse. He was very proud of his house and his family and especially proud of his beautiful daughter. When the time came for her to be married he decided that nobody he knew was good enough to be her husband. He wanted her to marry the strongest person on Earth.

'Go and ask the sun,' suggested Mrs Mouse. 'He must be the strongest person on earth. He can cross the world in a day. He ripens the crops in the field and the fruit on the trees. He keeps the world bright and warm and everybody likes him.'

'A good choice,' smiled Mr Mouse. 'We'll go and ask him right away.'

'Don't make me marry the sun,' said the mouse daughter to her mother. 'I'd rather marry another mouse.'

'Your father and I know what is best,' said Mrs Mouse. 'There isn't a mouse good enough to marry you, my dear.'

The mouse parents went to the sun and asked him if he'd like to marry their daughter.

'Yes, I would,' replied the sun. 'If you think I'm good enough for her.'

'Of course you are!' said Mrs Mouse. 'You're the strongest person in the world.'

‘Well,’ said the sun, ‘I have to tell you that I’m not as strong as the rain. When dark clouds cover the sky I have to go and hide my head. You don’t even know I’m there.’

‘In that case,’ said Mrs Mouse, ‘I’m afraid we can’t let you marry our daughter. Our son-in-law must be the strongest person in the world.’

‘We shall go and ask the rain instead,’ said her husband.

After a while the sky began to grow dark as the rain clouds gathered on the hill tops. Mr and Mrs Mouse went to speak to the rain.

'Yes, I'll marry your daughter,' said the rain. 'You were quite right to come to me. I am the most powerful person on Earth. Not only am I stronger than the sun but think what else I can do. Without rain nothing would grow. I can make huge rivers and waterfalls. I really am the most wonderful . . .'

At that moment a strong wind began to blow. It put a stop to the rain's boasting. 'Oh dear,' said the rain. 'I'm afraid I must be going. This wind is blowing me away.'

'Then I see you are not the best husband for our daughter,' sighed Mrs Mouse. 'If the wind can blow you away whenever he feels like it, he must be a stronger person than you.'

The strong wind came rushing across the fields. He blew the leaves off the trees and the birds about the sky. 'Stop!' shouted Mrs Mouse. 'We want a word or two with you.'

'Hurry up,' replied the wind, 'I'm in a rush. I have to go and dry some washing. Then I want to go and play with the boats on the sea.'

'You must be the strongest person in the world,' said Mrs Mouse.

'Not really,' replied the wind. 'That rock over there is stronger than I am. I've been trying to blow him over for hundreds of years but he won't move at all.'

'Oh dear,' groaned Mr Mouse. 'This isn't as easy as I thought it would be. I don't think we shall ever find anybody strong enough to marry our daughter. Tomorrow we will go and ask the rock. Whoever would have thought that he was stronger than the sun, the rain, and the wind.'

When they got home they told their daughter what had happened. 'I'm glad,' she said. 'I didn't want to marry the sun, nor the rain, nor the wind. I want to marry a mouse. In fact, I want to marry the handsome mouse who lives in the old barn.'

'Certainly not!' snapped her father.

'Out of the question!' said her mother. 'He's the poorest mouse we know. You must marry the strongest person on Earth, and that's the rock.'

The next morning Mr and Mrs Mouse got up early and went to speak to the rock.

'We understand that you are the strongest person in the world,' said Mrs Mouse, 'and we should be delighted if you would marry our daughter.'

'Kind of you to think of me,' replied the rock, 'but I'm afraid that I'm not the person for you. The black bull that lives in this field is stronger than I am. Every day he comes to sharpen his horns on me. Bits of me get chipped off as he does so. One day there will be nothing of me left. I think the black bull would make a better husband for your daughter.'

'I think the rock is right,' whispered Mrs Mouse. 'The black bull is very strong indeed. And he can move about. It would have been very annoying to have a son-in-law who could never come to visit us.'

By now the two mice were feeling rather foolish.

'Perhaps the best thing would be to let our daughter marry the mouse who lives in the barn,' suggested Mr Mouse.

'We're not giving up now,' replied Mrs Mouse. 'It was your idea to marry our daughter to the strongest person in the world and you're not going to change your mind. Go and talk to the black bull.'

The black bull was tied to an old rope in the cow-shed.

'We'd like you to marry our daughter,' said Mr Mouse.

'Nothing would give me greater pleasure,' replied the bull. 'I can't come just at the moment, I'm afraid, as you can see I'm tied up.'

'But we thought you were the strongest person in the world,' said Mrs Mouse. 'The rock told us you were.'

'Well, I am very strong,' answered the bull, 'but I'm not strong enough to break this old rope.'

'Old rope! Old rope!' yelled Mr Mouse. 'We can't marry our beautiful daughter to an old rope!'

'Be quiet!' said Mrs Mouse. 'The old rope may hear you, and be offended. Then he won't want to marry our daughter.'

'Excuse me, old rope,' said Mr Mouse wearily. 'Are you the strongest thing in the world?'

'Not quite,' answered the rope. 'I'm stronger than the black bull, as you can see, but every night a young mouse from the barn comes and gnaws at me. One day soon I shall be gnawed right through. Then I shall be good for nothing.'

'I knew it all the time,' laughed Mrs Mouse. 'That fellow from the barn must be the strongest person in the world. I can't think why we didn't ask him in the first place.'

The two young mice were delighted with the choice. They were married that very day and lived happily ever after.